MW00442845

Visit MascotBabies.com for everything Baby Sparty.

ISBN: 978-1-9831-8646-2

Text and illustrations copyright © 2019, Michigan State Publishing House.

Published in 2018 by Michigan State Publishing House, all rights reserved.

No portion of this book may be reproduced, stored in a retrieval system, or transmitted in any form or by any means, mechanical, electronical, photocopying, recording, or otherwise, without written permission from the publisher.

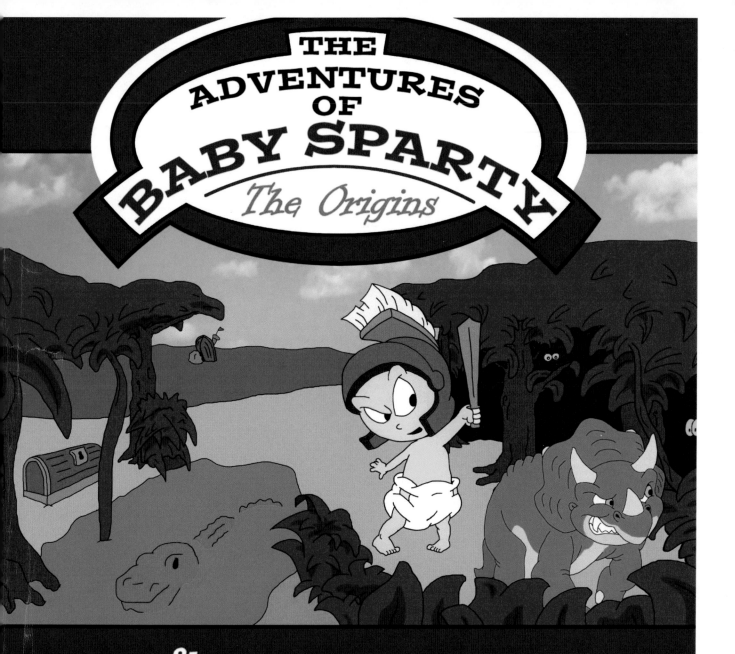

THE ADVENTURES OF BABY SPARTY

The Origins

Written & Illustrated by

Nicholas Fox

A long time ago, when the school was first founded.

They began construction for the first classroom.

The ground started shaking.

The sky grew dark and it began to rain and thunder.

He is the embodiment of MSU school spirit.

He is everything a great Spartan should be.

He is great at basketball.

An amazing football player.

He liked to play.

He liked to explore.

Baby Sparty was a role model and leader for the University.

The sword of Adventure.

By day, he would cheer on the school.

11779273R00017

Made in the USA
Monee, IL
17 September 2019